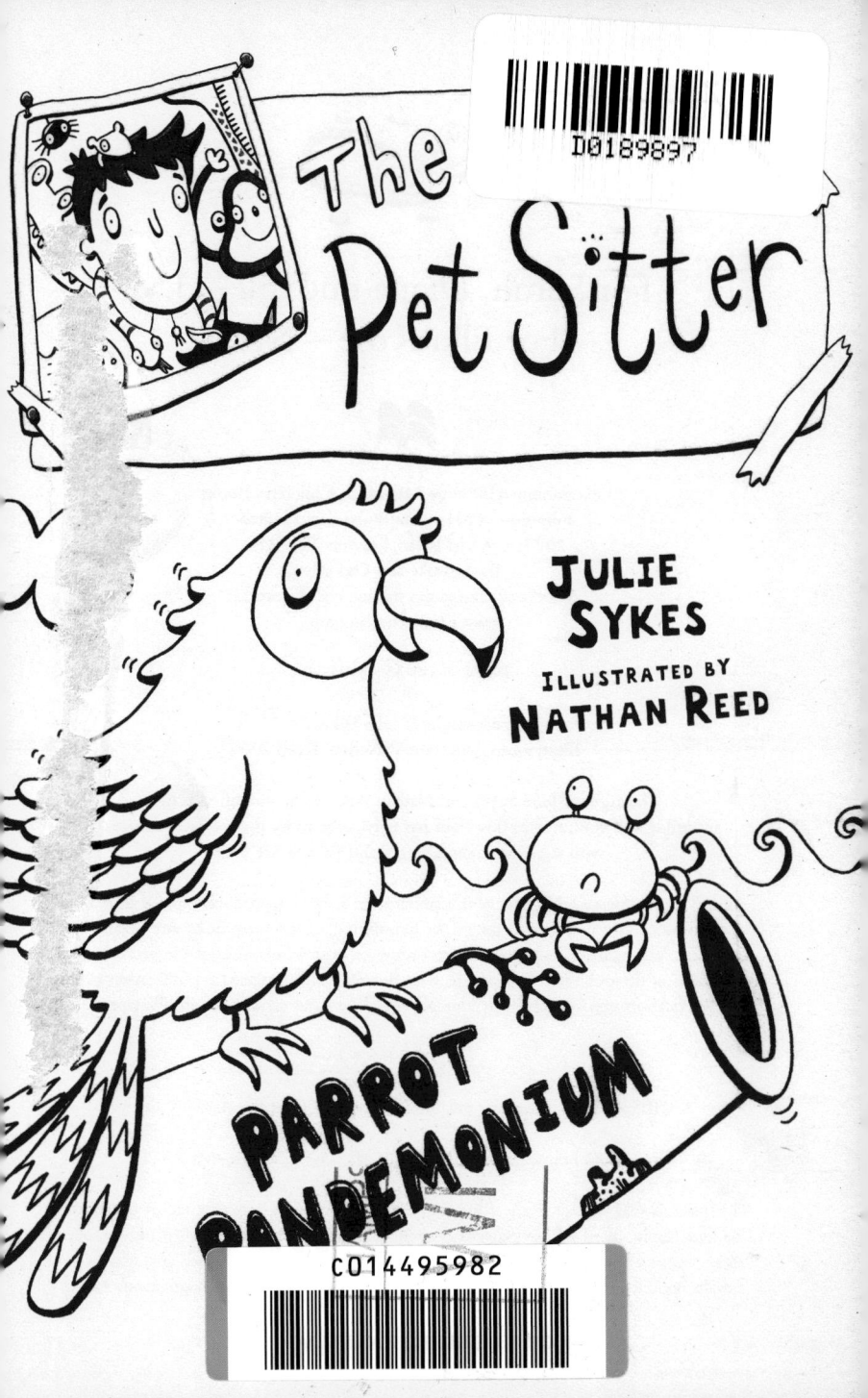

The Pet Sitter

Julie Sykes

ILLUSTRATED BY **Nathan Reed**

PARROT PANDEMONIUM

For Sarah, Diane and Jill – J.S.
For Ella Rose – N.R.

First published 2009 by Macmillan Children's Books
a division of Macmillan Publishers Limited
20 New Wharf Road, London N1 9RR
Basingstoke and Oxford
Associated companies throughout the world
www.panmacmillan.com

ISBN 978-0-330-51046-2

Text copyright © Julie Sykes 2009
Illustrations copyright © Nathan Reed 2009

The right of Julie Sykes and Nathan Reed to be identified as the
author and illustrator of this work has been asserted by them in accordance
with the Copyright, Designs and Patents Act 1988.

1 3 5 7 9 8 6 4 2

A CIP catalogue record for this book is available from the British Library.

Printed and bound in the UK by CPI Mackays, Chatham, ME5 8TD

CONTENTS

CHAPTER ONE
ANOTHER JOB

Max was on his way out to the garden when the telephone rang.

'I'll get it,' he said.

'It'll be for you anyway,' said Mum. 'It always is.'

Max snatched up the phone and was nearly deafened by the person on the other end.

'Is that Max Barker?'

'Yes,' said Max, hoping this was another job. Max was a pet sitter. He loved animals, but couldn't have any of his own because his big sister Alice was allergic to them.

1

'Hi, Max. My name's Captain Boom. I need a pet sitter to look after Squawk, my parrot. I'm going away tomorrow for two days, so could you come and meet him now?'

'Sure,' said Max, sticking his tongue out at Alice as she shoved past him. 'Where do you live?'

'At the Blue Water Marina, on a boat

called the *Leaky Dip*. You can't miss it. It's the oldest thing here apart from me.' Captain Boom laughed. 'How long will it take you to get here?'

'Ten minutes,' said Max.

'See you in ten minutes then,' said Captain Boom, hanging up.

Max quickly wrote Captain Boom's details in his pet sitter's notebook, then pulled on his trainers.

'Going somewhere?' asked Mum.

'Yes,' said Max. 'To the Blue Water Marina to meet Captain Boom. He wants me to look after his parrot.'

'But you don't know anything about parrots,' said Mum.

'I do,' Max replied. 'Alice is like a parrot. She squawks a lot and she's always repeating herself.'

'Muuuum! Tell him off!' squawked Alice.

Max grinned. 'See what I mean! Bye, Mum. Bye, Alice.'

'Be back by five,' called Mrs Barker.

As Max cycled to the marina he tried to imagine what Captain Boom would be like. He had a very loud voice for an old person. Would Squawk be old too? Max imagined an elderly bird with faded eyes and hardly any feathers.

'Pretty Polly,' he chirped, imitating the parrot in the local pet shop.

It didn't take long for Max to find the *Leaky Dip*. Captain Boom had been right; his boat was definitely the oldest one at the marina. Chaining his bike to a mooring ring, Max eyed the *Leaky Dip*'s gangplank. It was falling to pieces and didn't look very safe. Carefully he stepped

on to it. The gangplank creaked and Max waited a moment before taking another step forward. He was just taking a third step when someone bellowed, 'STOP!'

The voice was so fierce that Max immediately froze.

'Put your hands in the air.'

Max raised his arms. The rickety gangplank wobbled and he stared ahead, fixing his gaze on the *Leaky Dip*'s main mast to stop himself from losing his balance and falling into the sea.

'Walk forward, nice and slow. That's it. Now, lie face down on the deck.'

'What?' exclaimed Max. 'No way! I . . .'

'Do it!' roared the voice. 'Or I'll blow you to the other side of the world with a cannonball.'

CHAPTER TWO
ON BOARD THE LEAKY DIP

Max did as he was told, feeling his pet sitter's notebook slide out of his pocket as he lay down. He wanted to pick it up but he didn't dare. Being blown to the other side of the world wasn't on his agenda. Not today.

'Who are you?' snarled the voice. 'Why were you sneaking up my gangplank?'

'I'm Max Barker. I'm the pet sitter,' said Max, as clearly as he could with his mouth squashed against the deck's dusty surface.

'Of course you are!' said a deeper and much more friendly voice. 'Shiver me shoes, are you all right? I've been meaning to fix that gangplank for ages. Did you trip over the loose bit?'

Two strong hands hauled Max to his feet, and he found himself staring up at a huge man with bright blue eyes, a curly black beard and one hooped earring. Captain Boom must have been joking on the phone. He wasn't old at all and looked every bit a pirate. He was dressed in a white shirt, gold-buttoned waistcoat and raggedy three-quarter length trousers.

'Captain Billy Boom,' he said,

shaking Max's hand. 'Thanks for coming so quickly, and I'm really sorry about that gangplank. I'll fix it before I go, and that's a promise.'

'Er, great,' said Max, staring around to see who the other voice belonged to.

But apart from Captain Boom the deck was empty.

'Weird!' muttered Max, sure he hadn't imagined the other voice.

He rescued his notebook and flicked through until he found the right page.

'Captain Boom, the *Leaky Dip*, Blue Water Marina. Your parrot's called Squawk and you're going away for five days.'

'S'right.' Captain Boom sighed. 'It's Treasure trouble.'

'Bad luck,' said Max sympathetically.

'Did you forget where you buried it?'

Captain Boom roared with laughter.

'Not treasure,' he spluttered. 'Wish it was though. No, I'm going to visit Treasure. She's my sister, and believe me when I say she's trouble!'

'So is my big sister, Alice,' said Max. 'Is Treasure your big sister too?'

'You could say that. Think whale, then double it,' chuckled Captain Boom. 'But enough of Treasure. Come and meet Squawk.'

Captain Boom led the way across the deck, behind the mast and up five steps to the quarterdeck. Max followed, weaving his way around piles of frayed ropes, tattered sails and one very rusty cannon.

''Scuse the mess,' said Captain Boom. 'It never used to be like this. The clutter built up when the old boat sprung so many leaks that I had to stop sailing in her. I'll have a tidy up before I go, and that's a promise.'

Captain Boom stopped at a woody mast a bit smaller than the *Leaky Dip*'s main one and bellowed:

'Squawk, Max is here. Come down and say hello.'

Max squinted upwards and quickly realized something.

'That's not a mast; it's a tree!'

The tree looked like it had come straight from a tropical rainforest. Max ran his hand across its bark expecting it to be a fake, but the tree was real.

'Squawk,' shouted Captain Boom, 'come and meet Max.'

Shielding his eyes from the sun, Max stared between the tree's feathery leaves, hoping to catch a glimpse of Squawk. Nothing. The parrot stayed hidden.

'That's so cool!' said Max. 'A real tree growing on a

boat. I bet Squawk loves it.'

'S'right,' said Captain Boom. 'I got it when I got Squawk. Parrots and trees go together like sea and sand, maps and treasure, sharks and . . . SQUAWK! Get down from there right now. Don't think I can't see you!'

There was an angry screech from behind Max. He wheeled round in time to see a red blur hurtling towards him from the rigging of the main mast.

'Duck!' roared Captain Boom.

'It's not. It's definitely a parrot,' shouted Max, covering his head with his hands as the feathered cannonball hurtled closer.

CHAPTER THREE
SQUAWK SPEAKS

'Squawk, STOP!' roared Captain Boom. 'That's NOT funny. Behave yourself or I'll throw you in the bilge!'

The bird stopped mid-dive, skidding to a halt about a metre above the captain's head. Then, flying very slowly, he landed on Captain Boom's shoulder.

'Nice emergency stop,' said Max, impressed.

'Max, meet Squawk,' Captain Boom lightly stroked his parrot's beak. 'And, Squawk, meet Max, your pet sitter.'

'Hello, Squawk,' said Max.

Squawk fluffed up
his magnificent red, blue
and yellow feathers, then
stuck his beak in the air.

'Squawk,' said Captain Boom
with a note of warning, 'say hello to Max.'

Reluctantly Squawk fixed Max with his
small, black eyes.

'M . . . A . . . T,' he said, slowly. 'M-A-T.
Hello, Mat.'

'Max,' said Max and Captain Boom,
together.

'Mat,' repeated Squawk stubbornly.

'It's Max!' yelled Captain Boom.

'Mat,' said Squawk, giving Max a
hard stare. 'Mat. Cat. Cat, mat. The cat sat
on Mat.'

Max laughed.

'Very good,' he chuckled. 'A talking

parrot with a sense of humour.'

'Squawk's got a sense of humour all right,' said Captain Boom drily. 'And as for talking, he could talk the mainsail right off its mast. Ouch! Don't bite my ear. And while we're on the don'ts . . .' Captain Boom paused to make sure both Squawk and Max were listening. 'Don't let Squawk go anywhere near the mast. He loves it up there, but he's banned because he's a menace. He fiddles with the rigging and that causes accidents. And please DON'T upset my neighbour, Captain Becky Bones.'

Captain Boom pointed to a smart boat moored a short distance from the *Leaky Dip*. A skull and crossbones flew from each of its three masts, but not the usual type of skull and crossbones. Each of the skulls on Captain Becky Bones's flags had red blood oozing from their eye sockets. Max shivered and wished that Becky's boat was moored somewhere a bit further away, like Australia.

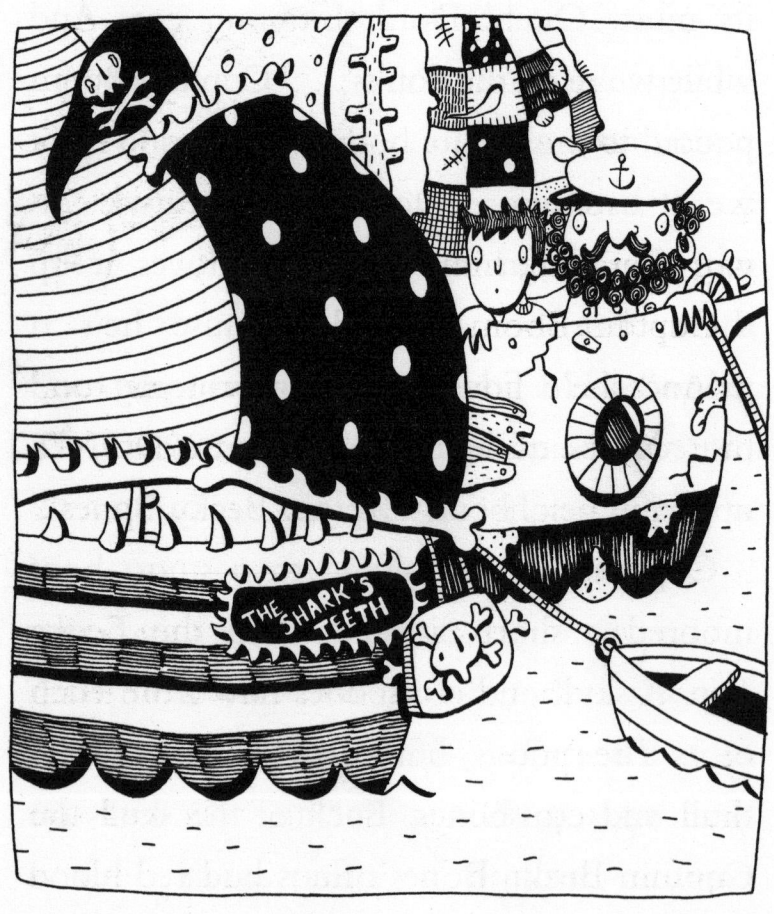

'Becky Bones, Captain of the *Shark's Teeth* and terror of the seas,' whispered Captain Boom. 'Upset her at your peril!'

Squawk crossed his eyes and made a gagging sound as if someone was strangling him.

Captain Boom grinned.

'And she'd have you for parrot pie too,' he said cheerfully. 'Right then, Max, let's step below and I'll show you what Squawk likes to eat.'

Leaving Squawk in his tree, Captain Boom climbed down a creaky ladder from the main deck. The space downstairs was even messier than up top. Gingerly Max followed the captain through a large cabin with a squashy sofa and small television and on into a tiny kitchen.

'This is the galley,' Captain Boom proudly announced.

Max squeezed in after him, nose wrinkled, expecting the worst, but the galley was spotlessly clean and tidy. Cooking utensils dangled from hooks on the wall, silver pans hung over a tiny cooker, and strings of garlic and onions hung around the porthole.

'I love cooking,' explained Captain Boom, patting his massive stomach. 'And Squawk and I both love eating.'

He pulled open a cupboard door and Max stared in amazement. The shelves were full of plastic containers, all neatly labelled in black pen.

'Walnuts, brazils, pecans, cashews,' read Max. 'Wheat, maize, sunflower, oats, linseed.'

'Squawk likes variety,' said Captain Boom, pulling open another door to reveal a fridge stashed with oranges, apples, grapes, cherries, mangoes, kiwi fruit, carrots, beans and much more. 'I'll write you a menu for each day. Make sure he has plenty of fresh water, and at bedtime he gets a treat of toast covered in honey, then cut into fingers and dipped in tea.'

'Not much then!' joked Max. 'Perhaps I'll move in here. All I get at bedtime is a lecture on cleaning my teeth.'

'Feel free,' said Captain Boom. 'I'll make a bunk up for you in the spare cabin before I go.'

Max laughed.

'Thanks, but I was only joking. Mum and Dad complain I'm never home as it is.'

'Well, the offer stands, if you change your mind,' said Captain Boom. He reached up, took a battered tin from a cupboard on the wall and shook its contents out. Max gaped at the tangle of jewellery, coins and notes that spilled over the work surface.

'How do you want to be paid? Jewellery or cash?' asked Captain Boom.

'Cash, please,' said Max quickly. 'I'm saving up for a new bike, and the shop only takes money.'

'Not very adventurous of it,' said Captain Boom.

'Tell me about it.' Max sighed. 'It does part exchange, but the man wouldn't even consider swapping my sister for the bike I want.'

Captain Boom laughed.

'I tried swapping Treasure once for Becky's third-best cannon. When Becky discovered Treasure was my sister she tied me to the mast and used me as a target to practise her knife-throwing trick.' Captain Boom shuddered. 'You don't mess with Captain Becky Bones!'

As Max left the *Leaky Dip* Becky Bones was sat on her deck peeling an orange with a sword. Seeing Max watching her, she suddenly threw the orange into the air. The sword flashed, then orange segments rained from the sky. Deftly Becky caught the pieces on the sword's blade and popped each one into her mouth.

'Phew,' said Max, hopping on to his bike and pedalling out of the marina. 'I'd rather arm-wrestle with an octopus than upset her!'

Chapter Four
A Cry for Help

Max couldn't wait to start his new pet-sitting job. The following morning, before breakfast, he went on the Internet to look for information on parrots.

'Parrots are noisy, sociable birds. They are quick to learn and are good mimics,' Max read. 'Pet parrots need challenging toys to stop them from getting bored. Climbing is a favourite pastime. They mustn't be left alone with furniture or electrical wires as they might damage them.'

There were lots of pictures of parrot toys, some of which reminded Max of the toys he'd had as a baby. Mum had kept all the favourite ones and, turning out the cupboard under the stairs, Max found his old wooden shape sorter.

'Squawk will love this,' he said, wiping off the dust.

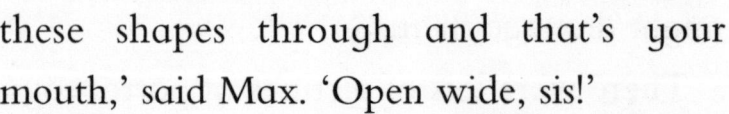

'What've you got there?' asked Alice, sneaking up behind him. 'Ooooh, do you need help, little Max? Can't you work out which shape goes through which hole?'

'There's only one hole big enough to fit these shapes through and that's your mouth,' said Max. 'Open wide, sis!'

'Hmph' snorted Alice. 'You're the one

with the big mouth. Watch what you say, Max, cos one day that mouth is going to get you into BIG trouble!'

'You wish!' said Max, slipping past Alice and going to put the shape sorter in a carrier bag, ready to take with him when he left to visit Squawk.

It was still early when Max arrived at the marina. No one was about as he chained his bike to a mooring ring. With the carrier bag in one hand Max stepped onto the *Leaky Dip*'s gangplank. If anything, the gangplank was even more wonky than it had been the day before.

'Captain Boom kept his promise to fix it then . . . not!' muttered Max.

'STOP!'

It was the same fierce voice that Max

had heard the day before, and once again he froze.

'Put your hands in the air.'

'What? No way. Look, I . . .'

BANG . . . WHOOOO . . . SPLASH!

Max never saw the cannonball, but it sounded very close and he immediately raised his hands above his head.

'That was just a warning,' said the scary voice. 'The next ball's got your name on it. So let's try again. Hands in the air and walk forward nice and slow.'

Slow as a sloth, Max inched his way along the gangplank until the voice called out again, 'Good. Now hop.'

'But—' squeaked Max.

'HOP!' roared the voice.

Max hopped, and his heart hopped too each time his foot left the rickety gangplank. Would he make it, or would he end up falling in the sea? Six agonizing hops later and Max was safely aboard the *Leaky Dip*. He risked a quick look round, but the deck was empty.

'STAND STILL!' roared the voice suddenly. 'What's in the bag?'

'A toy,' said Max, pulling out the shape sorter. 'It's for Squawk to play with. Squawk's a parrot. I'm—'

'I know who Squawk is! Squawk doesn't like toys for babies and nor do I. Next time bring sweets.'

'Sweets?' repeated Max in surprise.

'Jelly babies,' said the voice. 'So I can pull their heads off. Bring me jelly babies tomorrow or I'll pull your head off instead. Got that? Good. Now hop it.'

Max stared around but he could see no sign of the speaker. Was it safe to stay on the boat, or should he leave?

I've got to stay, Max decided. I can't leave Squawk here on his own.

Nervously Max crossed the main deck to the small aviary Captain Boom had shown him yesterday. Although Squawk was uncaged by day, Captain Boom insisted on locking him up at night.

'People steal parrots,' he'd told Max. 'They're worth a lot of money.'

Squawk was still asleep. Head tucked under one multicoloured wing, he was snoring loudly.

Max chuckled. He'd never heard of a snoring parrot.

'Squawk,' he called softly, 'wake up. It's Max. Your pet sitter.'

Squawk woke so quickly that Max suspected he hadn't been asleep at all. He wondered if Squawk had heard the strange voice and seen Max hopping up the gangplank. It was an embarrassing thought.

'Time for breakfast,' said Max, unlocking the aviary. 'It's mango this morning.'

'Hello, Mat,' said Squawk. 'Hello, door-mat.'

Max was thinking up a smart reply when a childlike cry made him spin round.

'Help!'

It sounded like a little girl, and it was coming from the top of the mast.

'Help!'

Screwing up his eyes against the morning sun, Max scanned the mast, but he couldn't see anyone there.

'Where are you?' he called.

'Up here.'

'Where? I can't see you.'

'I'm in the crow's nest.'

Max stared up to the special lookout post at the top of the mast. It was empty. The little girl must be very tiny if he couldn't see her over the top of its sides.

'Who are you? What are you doing up there?' shouted Max.

'I got lost. I thought if I climbed up high I might be able to see where I was going.'

'Come down,' said Max. 'Come down slowly and I'll help you find your way home.'

'I can't!' The voice rose to a squeal. 'I'm stuck! I'm too scared to move!'

'Ooooh!' Squawk stepped out of the aviary and waddled towards Max. 'Sounds like a job for me. I'll fly up and help her down, shall I?'

'Ha! So you *can* talk properly!' exclaimed Max. 'I knew it!'

Max was used to pet-sitting for talking animals, and Captain Boom had said that Squawk was a chatterbox.

'Course I can talk, bilge bucket! You

humans! You're all the same. You think you're the only ones born with a tongue!'

'Help!' called the little girl. 'I'm going to fall.'

'Quick! I'll go,' Squawk flapped his feathers as he prepared to take off.

'No!' said Max. 'You're not allowed up the mast. I'll go.'

'Spoilsport,' said Squawk. 'Well, don't go shouting for help when you get stuck too!'

'I won't,' said Max. 'I'm good at climbing.'

The mast was higher than it looked. Max climbed as fast as he dared while calling comforting words to the little girl, who was now crying. Reaching the crow's nest, Max sighed with relief. He'd made it! He raised his head over the top of the platform, kicked his legs and arrived in a heap. Quickly sitting up, Max stared round in surprise. The crow's nest was empty.

'Hello?' shouted
Max. 'Where are you?'

'Down here.' The
little girl dissolved
into giggles.

Crossly Max looked down at the deck. It
was like peering the wrong way through a
telescope. Everything was in miniature! The
splash of red, yellow and blue was Squawk.
That dirty white bundle was a pile of old
sails, the brown snake was a rope, and Max
could even see a broken oar. But there was
no sign of the little girl!

'Where down there?' shouted Max,
somewhat irritated.

'Here . . . And here . . . And here . . .
Over here . . . I'm here!'

The little girl's voice seemed to come at

Max from all directions. It echoed from down on the deck right up to the Jolly Roger at the very top of the mast. For a second Max wondered if he was losing the plot, then suddenly he got it! He'd been had! The voices and noises weren't real. None of them. Not the cannon fire, nor the scary voice that had forced him to hop up the gangplank. It was all a trick. And if he wasn't mistaken, Squawk was to blame.

'Parrots are good mimics,' Max remembered. 'And very good at throwing their voices too, by the sound of it!' he muttered.

Max started to laugh. 'Blazing beaks!' he exclaimed. 'I've been tricked by a parrot!'

CHAPTER FIVE
UPSETTING BECKY BONES

Max then heard Squawk's raucous cries of laughter. The parrot probably thought him a right nerdy-no-brain, falling for his tricks so easily!

Max gazed around, determined to make the most of the view before he climbed back down to the deck. He could see why Squawk liked playing on the mast. It was brilliant being so high up. It was also a great place for spying. Max could clearly see the *Leaky Dip*'s neighbour, the *Shark's Teeth*, and even in miniature she was a boat to admire.

'I'd love a ride on her,' said Max wistfully. 'I bet she's really fast.'

Max loved fast things. Unfortunately his parents didn't. Mum was the worst. She drove so slowly that even tractors overtook her! On board the *Shark's Teeth* a door burst open and Captain Becky Bones came running up on deck.

'Ahoy there, *Leaky Dip*,' she bellowed. 'Cut the noise. I'm trying to listen to the shipping news!'

Max chuckled softly as Squawk immediately stopped laughing. Then, to his horror, his own voice shouted back at Becky:

'Ahoy there, *Shark's Teeth*. Get a life. Listen to the Music Channel instead!'

Max whipped around, almost expecting to see his double sat behind him in the crow's nest. But of course there was nobody there. The voice had come from Squawk. He was mimicking Max and throwing his voice up to the top of the mast so it sounded like Max was doing the talking!

'What did you say?' Becky shook her fist skywards. 'Say that again and I'll have you for fish bait.'

'It wasn't me,' said Max, but his words were drowned out by his own voice calling, 'Fish bait yourself! You smell like it!'

'Squawk, stop it!'

Max had to shut Squawk up. Frantically he slithered down the mast. His legs snagged in the rigging and he got a splinter in his hand, but he didn't dare stop. Soon he was low enough to jump. He landed heavily, biting his tongue. Ignoring the pain, he hurtled across the main deck and threw himself at Squawk.

Squawk had been enjoying himself so much that he didn't see Max coming for him. 'Guuuuurrr, get off.'

'No way,' said Max, clamping Squawk's beak shut.

'Get off or I'll ring Parrotline,' mumbled Squawk. 'I know my rights.'

'What about *my* rights?' growled Max. 'My right not to end up as fish food.'

Keeping one hand firmly on Squawk's beak, Max called an apology to Becky Bones, then bundled Squawk below deck and into the galley.

'Like apologizing will help,' said Squawk smugly when Max let him go. 'Becky'll think you're a looney tune. Insulting her one minute, then apologizing the next. That was soooo funny! I'm a good mimic, aren't I?'

Max felt his lips twitch but he made them stay in a frown.

Squawk rubbed his head against Max's hand.

'I didn't mean to get you into trouble. I just got carried away.'

'Is that an apology?' asked Max.

'Yes,' said Squawk. 'Am I forgiven?'

'Only if you promise not to pull a stunt like that again,' said Max sternly. Then, unable to help himself, he burst into laughter.

Squawk laughed too, rolling on to his back and kicking his claws in the air until Max tickled his tummy. Then he righted himself fast!

'You can make it up to me by teaching me how to throw my voice,' Max suggested. I could use that trick at school! But now I'm going to cut up the mango Captain Boom left for your breakfast.'

'Bring me jelly babies tomorrow or I'll

pull your head off,' Squawk growled in the same fierce voice he'd used earlier.

'No more tricks,' said Max, slicing into the mango. 'Do you hear me?'

'No more tricks and that's a promise,' agreed Squawk, saluting Max with one wing.

CHAPTER SIX
AN ACCIDENT

The first day spent pet-sitting for Squawk was fun but exhausting! Max really liked the cheeky parrot, but he was very lively and barely stopped talking, even to breathe! Squawk didn't play any more tricks. Instead he taught Max how to project his voice, and by the end of the day Max was quite good at it.

'Bedtime, Squawk,' said Max. His voice sounded like it came from the rusty cannon.

'You're not going to lock me up, are you?' asked Squawk, swallowing his last piece of honey-coated toast.

'I am,' said Max.

'Why? I promise I'll be good. I won't go up the mast. I'll go and sleep in my tree.'

Squawk cocked his head and made sad eyes at Max.

'Don't!' exclaimed Max, feeling guilty. 'I have to lock you up. Captain Boom's worried you might get stolen.'

'Stolen!'

'Yeah!' Max chuckled. 'Anyone who stole you would soon bring you back! But that's not the point. I promised Captain Boom that I'd lock you up at night.'

'Like he keeps his promises,' said Squawk. 'His favourite saying is "That's a promise", but he never keeps any of them.'

'Oh,' exclaimed Max. 'So that's why he

didn't fix the gangplank!'

'S'right,' said Squawk. 'Captain Boom keeps promising to take me for a ride on a real boat – one that doesn't leak. But he hasn't done that yet either!'

'I'm sure he will,' soothed Max. 'Now please get into your aviary. It's bedtime, and I've got to go home for tea.'

Squawk waddled across the deck in his ungainly style, but stopped at the aviary door.

'Don't bother locking it,' he said. 'I can get out.'

'How?' asked Max.

Squawk tapped his beak with a wing.

'Like I'd tell you.'

'Promise me you won't do anything silly,' said Max.

'Like you care!'

'I do actually,' said Max. 'But then I've always had a soft spot for nutters!'

'Very funny, I'm sure' said Squawk, flapping into the aviary. 'Watch out, Max! I'll get you for that!'

'In your dreams,' said Max, padlocking the aviary door. 'And I hope they're sweet ones. Night, Squawk. See you tomorrow.'

Max slept so deeply he didn't hear his alarm ringing. The sun woke him, squeezing through a chink in the curtains. Leaping out of bed, Max pulled on his clothes.

'Squawk is not going to be happy with me,' he panted as he raced for the bathroom.

Alice was in there, and no amount of banging on the door would shift her. Max gave up on a wash, waved a comb at his unruly hair, grabbed a piece of toast from the rack on the table and bolted out to the shed to get his bike. He pedalled to the marina so fast his tyres almost smoked. He didn't slow down until he'd chained his bike to the *Leaky Dip*'s mooring ring and was halfway up the gangplank. Then he stopped dead. The gangplank was wobbling ominously.

'Not so fast,' he told himself.

Slowly Max took one step. The gangplank groaned. Max waited for it to settle, then took another careful step. This time the gangplank juddered then suddenly plunged into the water, tipping Max in too. 'Urrrgh!' Max gasped in surprise.

He trod water for a moment to get his bearings. He was halfway between the

Leaky Dip and the shore. Max was deciding which way to swim when the gangplank floated up behind him and bopped him on the head. He spluttered, sank under the water and when he surfaced a long strand of seaweed was stuck to his face. Max thought he heard a giggle, but he was too busy trying to stay afloat to wonder about it. His clothes and trainers were full of water, and the extra weight was pulling him down.

Panting like a dog, Max struck out for the *Leaky Dip*. But he hadn't realized how high the boat's deck was above the sea's surface. He couldn't quite reach it, and with each failed attempt he swallowed another mouthful of salty water.

'Hang on!' called a voice.

Max heard something whizzing through the air, then felt another blow to the back of his head. It pushed him under and when he surfaced again, coughing up more water, he found his arms were pinned to his sides.

'Argh!' Max yelped.

He struggled fiercely until he realized he was fighting with a life ring. Wriggling like a caterpillar, he squeezed first one arm and then the other over the top of the ring.

'Hurray!'

From the handrail of the *Leaky Dip* Squawk cheered wildly.

'Squawk! How did . . . ?' Max broke off, suddenly realizing that the current was pulling him towards the *Shark's Teeth*.

CHAPTER SEVEN
A PROPER PROMISE

'**E**r, morning,' Max called out politely.

Becky Bones was only little, but her loud voice made up for her slight frame.

'What do you think you're playing at?' she bellowed.

'Erm, I'm having a wash,' said Max, splashing water over his face. 'I'm running late this morning, there was a queue for the bathroom—'

'This is a marina,' Becky cut in angrily, 'not a hotel. I'm trying to practise my sword dance and you're distracting me. I nearly chopped my toe off just then. Come any closer and I'll make you walk the plank.'

'Nice to meet you too,' muttered Max, frantically kicking his skinny legs against the current as he fought his way back to the *Leaky Dip*.

'Go, Max,' yelled Squawk excitedly.

The parrot moved down and began pulling at something on the deck. Suddenly a bundle of rope slithered over the side and into the water.

'Yo!' screeched Squawk as the rope ladder unfolded.

Gratefully Max reached out and climbed aboard the *Leaky Dip*. Water gushed from him, and a shell fell out of his trainers when he pulled them off.

Squawk hopped up and

down the handrail screeching with laughter.

'That was a good one!' he shouted. 'That was my best ever.'

'What do you mean?' asked Max coldly. 'And how did you get out of your aviary?'

'Told you I could!' Squawk stopped laughing and looked smug. 'It's easy. I picked the lock. But I didn't expect you to fall in. That was wild!'

'What do you mean?'

'The gangplank joke. It wasn't meant to fall in the water. Just slip a little to give you a fright.'

'You set me up? But you promised there'd be no more tricks.'

'We don't keep promises on the *Leaky Dip*,' said Squawk.

'Well, it's about time you did, shrimp face!' spluttered Max. 'You could have drowned me.'

'Keep your feathers on,' said Squawk calmly. 'You sound like Becky Bones. It was a joke. No harm done.'

'No harm done?! Look at me,' said Max.

'So you're a bit wet! What's the big deal? You can borrow something to change into. Captain Boom's got tons of clothes,'

'That's OK then,' said Max sarcastically, 'cos we're easily the same size, aren't we?'

Squawk's face fell. 'Oooh, I didn't think of that. Never mind. You'll soon dry in the sun, and there's a good sea breeze.'

Max glared at Squawk, thinking of all the horrible things he'd like to do to the parrot to get his own back. Then he heard his own voice repeating:

'I'm having a wash. I'm running late this morning, there was a queue for the bathroom.'

Then Becky's rougher tones answered,

'This is a marina, not a hotel.'

Squawk was so good at mimicking Becky
that Max couldn't help but laugh. And once
he'd started laughing he saw the funny side
of Squawk's joke and he laughed even
more. Squawk joined in. He lay on his back
and, kicking his claws in the air, laughed
hysterically. Max tried that too, kicking his
legs in the air, until, remembering his pet-

sitting duties, he sat up.

'I'll go and get your breakfast. I think it's oats with linseed oil and kiwi fruit today.'

'Yum, yum,' said Squawk. 'I'll just sit here in the sun and let you wait on me then.'

'Fine,' said Max. 'But no more tricks, OK?'

'I promise,' said Squawk.

'A proper promise, not a *Leaky Dip* one?'

'A proper promise,' agreed Squawk. 'Don't be long. I'm starving!'

Max squelched down to the galley to prepare Squawk's breakfast. He peeled and sliced the kiwi fruit, then arranged it over the oats. Next he drizzled linseed oil on top. Pleased with his efforts, Max carried the dish of food back on deck to Squawk.

'Yummy,' said Squawk, swiping a piece of kiwi fruit before Max had even put the dish down. 'I'm starving.'

'Slow down,' laughed Max. 'You'll make yourself sick.' While Squawk gobbled his breakfast Max tidied up the aviary. Then he nipped down to the galley to refill Squawk's bowl of water.

As Max stepped back on deck the *Leaky Dip* rolled suddenly. Max wobbled, almost spilling the water. Carefully he made his way back to the aviary. The wind was getting up, and Max's wet clothes flapped uncomfortably. Someone was shouting. It sounded like Becky Bones. Max grinned, glad he wasn't getting a telling-off this time. The shouting grew louder. Then there was a tremendous *bang!* The *Leaky Dip* shuddered so violently that Max fell head first into the aviary and dropped the water bowl on his toe.

'Ouch!' he yelled, shaking his wet foot. 'Squawk, what are you doing now?'

It sounded like the parrot was messing about with the old cannon. Max legged it back to the main deck but Squawk was no where near the cannon. He was staring at the *Shark's Teeth*. On board, Captain Becky Bones was leaping in the air.

'Come back here,' howled Becky, waving her sword at Max.

'Yeah, right,' whispered Max. 'So you can cut us up and feed us to the fish. I don't think so. What's she cross about this time?'

'Can't you guess?' Squawk's tiny eyes were bright with fear and Max realized he was missing something.

'Guess what?'

'We just crashed into the *Shark's Teeth* and put a dent in the side.'

'What? How could we?'

'Because no one's steering the boat,' said Squawk.

'What are you talking about? You don't steer a boat that's tied up in a marina.'

'But we're not,' whispered Squawk.
'We've come adrift. We're heading out
to sea.'

CHAPTER EIGHT
SQUAWK AT SEA

Squawk hung his head.

'It was an accident,' he mumbled. 'I think I untied the wrong rope when I was setting up the gangplank trick.'

'Great,' said Max. 'I feel much better now I know you didn't mean to do it.'

'Really?'

'No,' said Max. 'Remind me – where is the ship's wheel?'

'Over there,' said Squawk, pointing a multicoloured wing at a large wooden wheel on the main deck. 'But . . .'

As Max ran to the ship's wheel he tried to

remember how to steer a boat. He'd done it once before, on holiday. It wasn't like steering a bicycle or a car. You had to turn the wheel and wait for the wind to take you where you wanted to go. The *Leaky Dip*'s wheel was as battered as the rest of the ship. Carefully Max grasped it between his skinny hands and turned it to the left. Nothing happened. Perhaps it took even longer to turn this type of boat?

Max hung on, willing the boat to turn. When it didn't, he spun the wheel round further.

'It doesn't work very well,' said

Squawk, flying over. 'It's broken. Captain Boom's never bothered to fix it because the *Leaky Dip* has too many holes to go sailing in her.'

'Have you got *any* good news?' snapped Max.

'Er, I don't expect we'll get that far. Not without a sail.'

'We've drifted quite a way already,' said Max, looking back at the marina. 'The current's pulling us. We're going to have to put the sail up or we'll never get back. We'll just drift further out.'

Squawk brightened. 'Does that mean I get to go up the mast?'

Max did some quick thinking. He couldn't be in two places at once, and it would probably be safer to let Squawk put the sail up than let him steer the boat. The wheel was heavy, and Max doubted Squawk would be able to turn it.

'OK, but no tricks. You put the sail up and come straight back. This is serious, Squawk. We could drown if you mess around.'

Squawk looked offended.

'I'm not an airhead,' he said gruffly.

'No, you're a birdbrain,' chuckled Max. 'Now go and get that sail up. We're almost out on the open sea.'

Enthusiastically Squawk flew off to unfurl the mainsail. Max, a hand shielding his green eyes from the sun, watched as the bird untied each of the ropes that bound the sail to the mast. But his relief was short-lived. As the sail began to unfold, Max saw it was full of holes. When Squawk finally returned to the deck Max couldn't help commenting, 'It's more string vest than sail.'

Squawk groaned, then tucked his head under his wing.

'It wasn't that funny,' said Max.

'Not laughing,' moaned Squawk. 'I don't feel well. I feel sick.'

'You probably ate your breakfast too fast,' said Max, unsympathetically.

'I always eat that fast,' said Squawk. 'This is different. I feel awful. Stop the boat from going up and down!'

'So sorry, I'll try and find a flat bit of sea!'

Experimentally Max wiggled the ship's wheel.

'No, can't find any flat bits. It's got something to do with these pesky waves!' he said with even more sarcasm.

'I'm going to be . . .' Squawk lurched forward and was sick all over Max's shoe.

'*Gross!*' thought Max, then, remembering he was the pet sitter, he pulled a very damp tissue from his pocket and carefully wiped Squawk's beak.

'Better now?'

'Noooooo,' moaned Squawk. 'Not better. I want to go back. Don't like it out here. The sea's too wonky.'

'You get seasick?' Max was incredulous. 'Whoever heard of a pirate's parrot suffering from seasickness?'

'Runs in the family,' Squawk whimpered. 'My uncle ran away with a circus cos the sea makes him so ill.'

'Do you want to go and sit in your tree? I'll carry you there if you like.'

'Noooo,' groaned Squawk. 'I want to lie down.'

'Shall I make you a bed then?'

'Yes, please.'

Max looked at the junk around him. There was plenty here to make Squawk a comfortable bed. With one hand still on the ship's wheel Max stretched out and managed to pull a battered old crate towards him. Then, hooking a piece of sailcloth over his foot, he lifted that over too. The sailcloth fitted perfectly inside the crate. Max quickly let go of the ship's wheel to help Squawk into his new bed.

'Is that better?'

'Yes,' said Squawk, 'but I wouldn't mind a drink of water.'

Max looked around. They'd safely passed all the boats in the marina and had almost reached the open sea. Max knew a little about wind and how it affected the direction a boat could take. Once out at sea Max hoped to sail the *Leaky Dip* in a circle to bring her back to the marina. At the speed they were travelling, he probably had enough time to nip down to the galley and get Squawk some water before he made the turn.

'I'll be one second,' he said.

Faster than a galleon in a gale Max raced to the galley. He filled a bowl with water, then rushed back to find Squawk had fallen asleep.

'Great,' said Max. He was thirsty himself now, but he didn't dare leave the ship's wheel again. The *Leaky Dip* was already drifting away to the left. Max fixed his eye on a red buoy and steered towards it. At first the boat didn't seem to respond, but after a while Max was happy they were travelling in the direction he wanted to go. Enviously he watched a sleek boat coming up fast behind the *Leaky Dip*. The boat had three masts, each with a pennant flying from the top. Max squinted at the pennants, trying to work out what was on them. A sudden boom made him jump. Something whistled through the air and splashed into the sea a short way from the *Leaky Dip*.

'Snapping sharks!' exclaimed Max.

Now the boat was closer he could clearly see its three pennants. Each had a skull and crossbones, with red blood oozing from the eye sockets.

There was another bang and Max ducked as a cannonball hurtled from one of the six gleaming cannons on board. Amazingly the cannonball splashed into the sea, missing the *Leaky Dip* by a shrimp's leg.

'Oh no!' groaned Max, a cold feeling stealing over him. 'It's the *Shark's Teeth*, and I don't think Becky Bones is trying to invite me to lunch.'

Chapter Nine
The Battle

The noise woke Squawk. Woozily he sat up and was sick over Max's other shoe.

'Nice,' sighed Max. 'A matching pair!'

'Water,' quavered Squawk. 'I need a drink.'

Max quickly let go of the ship's wheel to push Squawk's water bowl closer. The parrot took a few sips, then leaned against Max's leg.

'How are you feeling now?' he asked.

'Sick as a parrot,' moaned Squawk.

Max stroked the parrot's head. He didn't like seeing him in this state. He preferred

Squawk the joker.

'We'll soon be home,' he said, sneakily glancing back at the *Shark's Teeth*.

The rival boat was approaching fast. Max could see Captain Becky Bones furiously waving her sword at the *Leaky Dip*. She shouted something that Max couldn't hear. Max willed the *Leaky Dip* on, but if anything she seemed to be slowing down. Max knew his only chance was to get back to the marina. It should be busy there by now. Too busy for Captain Bones to carry out her worst threats. But out here on the open sea Max could be made to walk the plank and only the fish would know! Were there sharks this close to the shore? Max shivered. He didn't know and he didn't want to find out!

'Squawk,' said Max casually, 'where does Captain Boom keep his cannonballs?'

'Under his bunk,' said Squawk. 'Why?'

'Erm,' Max hesitated, not sure how much to tell Squawk when he was so unwell.

'Becky Bones is after us, isn't she?'

Max laughed. Squawk was too clever for his own good!

'Yes.'

'S'good, said Squawk, closing his eyes. 'She'll soon put me out of my misery!'

'That's not going to happen,' said Max. 'We'll be back in the marina soon, and then you'll feel better.'

He glanced at the *Shark's Teeth* again. The boat was definitely gaining on the *Leaky Dip*. Max didn't have any option.

He would have to leave the wheel in order to fetch a supply of cannonballs. Gently he lifted Squawk back into his makeshift bed.

'Stay there,' he said.

'Like I'm going anywhere else,' muttered the parrot.

Once again Max raced below deck. Captain Boom's cabin was easily the messiest place on board ship. Max waded through dirty clothes, towels and a mountain of *Pirate Weekly* magazines until he reached the bunk. He scrabbled around underneath it, pulling out more junk until he found what he was looking for. A rusty iron ball a bit smaller than a football.

'Is that it?' muttered Max, feeling under the bunk again. 'There must be more than one.'

But there wasn't. Disappointed, Max

carried the cannonball back on deck. The *Shark's Teeth* was much closer now. The moment Max took hold of the *Leaky Dip*'s wheel Becky Bones started shouting at him again. Max closed his ears and concentrated on steering the boat back towards the harbour.

They were making very slow progress. The *Leaky Dip* groaned and leaned sharply to the right. Max hung on to the wheel and used his foot to stop Squawk's bed from sliding away. Then Max noticed the water. The deck was like a paddling pool. Max, whose trainers were still wet after his early-morning swim, was shocked that he hadn't noticed the flooded deck before.

'Snapping sharks!' he exclaimed. 'We're sinking.'

'Man the lifeboat,' said Squawk weakly.

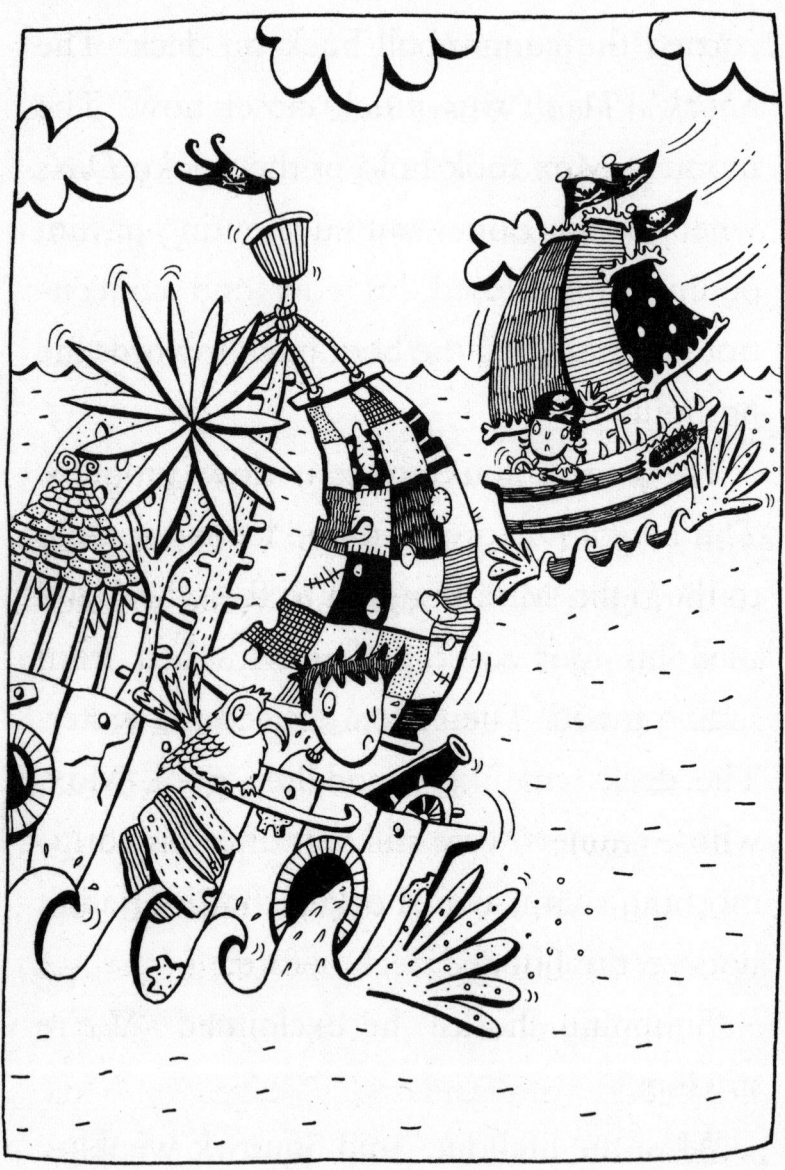

Max brightened.

'Good idea. Where is it?'

'There isn't one. Captain Boom keeps promising to buy one, but . . .' Squawk shrugged his wings.

'Another *Leaky Dip* promise,' sighed Max.

As fast as the *Leaky Dip* was filling up with water, so the *Shark's Teeth* was getting closer. Max gave up trying to steer while he prepared the cannon.

'We're going down fighting,' he said.

'Matches in the locker over there,' said Squawk.

Luckily the water hadn't reached the locker. Pocketing the matches, Max loaded the cannonball and took aim. The *Shark's Teeth* drew alongside the *Leaky Dip*. Max heard scrabbling, like an enormous rat, then

Captain Becky Bones climbed up over the handrail, a rope in her mouth.

'Hold your fire,' she said with her mouth full.

'Yeah, right!' muttered Max, lighting the match.

There was a muffled bang, followed by a small thud. A thick cloud of black dust burst from the end of the cannon. Then the cannon ball plopped out and rolled across the *Leaky Dip*'s wet deck. Max coughed and wiped the dust from his eyes. Typical! Even the cannon didn't work properly.

'I should have guessed,' groaned Max, wishing he'd thought to arm himself. Even a frying pan would have been better than nothing. But it was too late now.

'Shiver me shoes!' roared Captain Becky

Bones, leaping aboard. 'What part of hold your fire didn't you understand?'

Deftly she tied the *Shark's Teeth*'s mooring rope to a ring on deck, then, spitting on her hand, she rubbed at her sooty face.

'I don't know why I'm bothering to rescue you,' she said fiercely.

Max stared in amazement. He was so scared that his brain was having trouble working everything out.

'Rescue us? But you've just tried to sink us with cannonballs.'

'That was to get your attention. I'd have hit you if I'd wanted to.'

'You've really come to save us?'

'Yes,' growled Becky Bones, as if she hadn't really wanted to. 'Your boat's dangerous. It's too full of holes to sail anywhere.'

'But why would you help us?'

'I owe Captain Boom a favour. When I accidentally cut off my finger, practising sword moves, Captain Boom drove me to hospital, where a clever doctor sewed it back on. See?' Proudly Becky Bones showed Max a wonky finger with a neat scar at its base.

'Captain Boom always seems a little scared of me, but I couldn't let the *Leaky Dip* sink. I might not get such a helpful neighbour next time.'

Max grinned with relief. 'That's lucky.'

'It will be if we make it back. You're not out of the water yet!' Becky Bones laughed at her own joke. 'Better get a move on before I change my mind and leave you to sink!'

Chapter Ten
One More Promise

The journey back to the marina was long and slow. Even under tow, Max still had to steer the *Leaky Dip* while baling out the water at the same time. He also had to take care of Squawk. But once they were safely back in their old mooring the sick parrot quickly perked up, until Becky produced a list of chores she wanted doing to make up for the dent in the *Shark's Teeth*.

'Sick as a parrot,' wailed Squawk when Max told him their first job was to scrub the decks.

'You'll be sicker than a parrot if you

don't lend a wing,' said Max sternly. 'I'll lock you in your aviary, and this time I'll use the padlock from my bicycle chain. It's a number combination so you won't be able to pick that!'

'Huh! You're harder than Becky's Bones!' joked Squawk.

'What's that about my bones?'

Squawk jumped guiltily, but there was no one there.

'What . . . ?'

Max grinned.

'Get a move on bird brain,' he said in Becky's gruff voice.

Squawk laughed.

'Nice one, Max. You had me fooled.'

'Good,' said Max. 'But no more jokes. It's time to work.'

Squawk and Max sat on a branch in Squawk's tree, watching for Captain Boom, who was due home any minute.

'There he is,' shouted Squawk excitedly as a battered car pulled up next to the *Leaky Dip*'s gangplank. 'Last one down's a dodo.'

Squawk launched himself from the branch and flew

towards the gangplank. Max slithered down the tree trunk. He was miles behind Squawk, but still in time to see Captain Boom stumble on the wonky gangplank and almost fall into the sea.

'I'll fix that today, and that's a promise,' puffed Captain Boom as he stepped on deck. 'Hello, you two. How did it go?'

'Good, thanks,' said Max. 'How was Treasure?'

'Same as usual. How was Squawk?'

'He was good.'

'Really?!' Captain Boom sounded surprised. 'What – no tricks, no jokes? He didn't upset Captain Becky Bones even once?'

'Erm, Squawk was Squawk,' said Max, truthfully.

Captain Boom stared at Squawk, and Squawk stared innocently back.

'So you'd look after him again?'

'Yes, I'd definitely pet-sit for you again.' Max winked at Squawk. 'And that's a promise!'

Me and Squawk

ABOUT THE AUTHOR

Julie Sykes has had more than thirty books published including several about her creation, Little Tiger. Among her other titles are *That Pesky Dragon*, *Dora's Eggs* and *Hurry, Santa!*

I Don't Want to Go to Bed! and *I Don't Want to Have a Bath!* won the Nottingham Children's Book Award. Julie has three children and lives in Hampshire.

ABOUT THE ILLUSTRATOR

Nathan Reed has illustrated children's stories for Puffin, HarperCollins and Campbell Books. He also illustrated one of the most popular titles in Kingfisher's *I Am Reading* series, *Hocus Pocus Hound*. Nathan lives in London.

A selected list of titles available from Macmillan Children's Books

The prices shown below are correct at the time of going to press. However, Macmillan Publishers reserves the right to show new retail prices on covers, which may differ from those previously advertised.

All Pan Macmillan titles can be ordered from our website, www.panmacmillan.com, or from your local bookshop and are also available by post from:

Bookpost, PO Box 29, Douglas, Isle of Man IM99 1BQ
Credit cards accepted. For details:
Telephone: 01624 677237
Fax: 01624 670 923
Email: bookshop@enterprise.net
www.bookpost.co.uk
Free postage and packing in the United Kingdom